McTans

COLOUR JETS

KU-005-278

The FOOTPRINTS Mystery

Andrew Donkin and Jeff Cummins

Collins

COLOUR JETS

With love for Camille and Olivia Chevallier
(and special thanks to S.R.E.P.)

First published in Great Britain by HarperCollins Publishers Ltd 1997

10 9 8 7 6 5 4 3 2 1

Text © Andrew Donkin 1997
Illustrations © Jeff Cummins 1997

The author and illustrator assert the moral right
to be identified as the author and illustrator of the work.

A CIP record for this title is available from the British Library.

ISBN 0 00 675289-6

Chapter 1
More Footprints

The mystery was getting bigger all the time.

Four weeks ago people in the town started finding trails of footprints. The footprints always appeared at night. Nobody ever saw what made them.

It was an enigma.
A puzzle. A riddle.

MYSTERY FOOTPRINTS

MORE FOOTPRINTS FOUND

CREATURE ON THE LOOSE!

TRACKER CALLED IN!

I had read all the reports.
I'd pinned all the cuttings
on my notice board.
This was *my* mystery.

It was Saturday. As soon as I woke up I raced down to the kitchen. On the table, between a pile of toast crumbs and a soggy cornflake, was the morning paper.

RADCLIFFE CHRONICLE

SLEEPY GARDENER GETS SHOCK IN FLOWERBED!

New footprints had appeared – and I had the whole weekend to investigate.

Most people thought that the footprints were being made by a big cat. Maybe it was a lion or a tiger that had escaped from the zoo.

The Mayor had even called in Rupert Smugg, a professional tracker.

RUPERT SMUGG

TRACKER OF STRANGE
AND FABULOUS BEASTS

He had the kind of face you want to throw mud at.

I had to get moving straight away, before the trail went cold.

The mystery was growing all the time and I had to solve it before he did. Rupert Smugg – the enemy.

Chapter 2
Into the Mystery

I'd been following the footprints case since the very beginning. Nobody knew more about it than me.

I had mapped the location of every trail and talked to the people who'd found them.

The latest tracks were in the garden of Mrs Rogers, 28 Budoch Drive.

I'm with the *Radcliffe Chronicle*…

…which was true. I had a copy in my pocket.

Mrs Rogers muttered something about reporters getting younger all the time and took me into the garden.

It's ruined my roses. Trampled my tulips. And destroyed my daffs.

I examined the footprints while Mrs Rogers waffled on about her plants. This was the longest set of tracks yet.

I checked my map. They headed east towards the old library.

The building had been knocked down about a month ago. The whole site was just rubble now and it would be the perfect hiding place.

I thanked Mrs Rogers and headed for the library. The answer could be lurking in the ruins.

Chapter 3
The Hunt

The area where the library had stood was going to be a car park, but the rubble hadn't been cleared yet.

Inside were more footprints.
Lots of footprints. I was getting closer.

I crept through the piles of broken bricks and fallen stones. The place smelled damp and musty.

Then I heard a noise. Around the corner, something was hiding. My stomach lurched.

My camera was ready. My finger was right on the button.

It was Rupert Smugg. He had followed
the trail to the library as well.

I knew that he knew that I knew what
we were really looking for.

"No point in sticking around this dump now," he said, narrowing his eyes.

It was obvious we weren't going to be best friends. Smugg left in a huff.

I got the impression he was a five-huff-a-day man.

Now Rupert had gone my heart finally stopped jumping. I thought that was going to be all the excitement for today.

Afternoon, chuck!

It wasn't.

Chapter 4
The Gargoyle Wakes

One of the pieces of fallen stonework was shining like a rainbow working overtime. The dull grey stone was becoming bright flesh.

It was the creature. The footprints-creating, plant-breaking, mystery-making creature.

I gulped very loudly.

GULP!

I was the library's gargoyle... until they knocked it down.

"They smashed everything to pieces," he said. He sounded very miserable and his eyes glowed a sad blue.

I thought about the photograph of the old library. Funny – I had never really noticed the gargoyle before.

The gargoyle's skin looked scaly and bright like a lizard's. I wanted to touch it.

Now I've got no home. Every time I look for a new one, I get people trying to track me.

I felt a bit guilty because I'd been sort of hunting him as well.

"I'll help you," I said, although I didn't have a clue how.

"I don't think anyone can help me," he replied. And with that he turned back into cold stone. Just another piece of unwanted rubble.

I waited around for a while, but he didn't move again.

Chapter 5
Books are Useful

As soon as I got home, I looked up gargoyles in a book.

GARGOYLES

Stone gargoyles began appearing on buildings during medieval times. There are many different forms of gargoyles. They are believed to act as guardians of their chosen buildings.

So, the gargoyle needed a new place to live. It's horrible when you have to move. I know – we did it when Dad got a new job.

I wanted to help, but I didn't know how. I started looking things up – gargoyles, ancient buildings, cities.

I found the answer just before supper.

Chapter 6
A Good Plan

Next morning I raced back to the library.

I held the book open in front of the gargoyle. His eyes turned a piercing green as he scanned the pages.

Look!

Other gargoyles?

Yes, in the city. We should go there. They could help find you a new home. It's only an hour on the train.

Before the gargoyle could answer, we heard a truck pull up outside.

It was Smugg, back on the hunt.

The gargoyle told me to climb on his back. His skin was soft and smooth, like thick velvet.

Hang on tight.

A gust of wind came from nowhere and carried us upwards.

Behind me I heard Rupert Smugg running towards us.

But there was nothing he could do.

CRACK!

We were clean away.

Chapter 7
Skylarking

The town fell away below us until it looked like a nest of tiny ants. The wind whooshed past and made my ears feel as cold as ice.

Higher! Go higher!

The gargoyle caught an updraught with his massive wings. We sailed up into the open blue sky.

I ate my sandwiches sitting on the back
of a gargoyle flying five hundred metres
in the air.

I gave him a big piece of crust.
It seemed only fair.

We flew all afternoon
and turned left at the white horse.

Ahead of us was a huge dark cloud.
It growled with hidden thunder. I wanted
to see inside it.

Can we go through it?

It was like flying into a bucket of cold
water. My hands got wet and slippery.
So did the gargoyle's back. I tried to
hang on, but the wind was too strong.

I fell off.

Chapter 8
It Never Rains but it Pours

I dropped like a stone.

A great big,

heavy,

huge,

stupid

stone.

The ground raced up like it had really missed me while I'd been away.

Behind me I heard the sound of powerful wings all mixed up with thunder from the clouds.

I closed my eyes and felt a claw dig into the back of my coat.

I thought I told you to hang on!

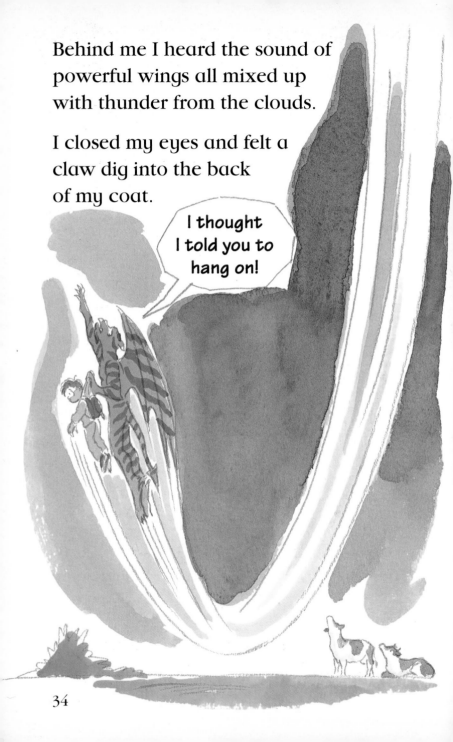

Then the storm clouds burst. Cold drops
of rain hit us hard. I wiped my face.

The downpour was much too heavy to
fly through.

I checked my compass
and we headed west.

Chapter 9
Help

By the time we reached the city the rain had eased off. After the storm the day smelled fresh and new.

Afternoon.

I was seeing things differently. I think it was because I was with the gargoyle.

We found the building I'd seen in the book and flew up on to the roof. There was the trio of small gargoyles.

When they stopped arguing we explained why we'd come to the city.

"Stone me," said the middle gargoyle. "You'd better go and see Demnos at the museum. He's in charge of the buildings around here."

"He'll sort you out," they agreed. Then they started arguing again.

To get to the museum we had to travel over the rooftops of the city. It was the only way to avoid being seen.

Chapter 10
The Museum

By now it was late afternoon and the museum had just closed. We got inside through a skylight.

The air was thick with dust and history. You could taste the centuries on your tongue.

We sneaked around the Egyptian mummies…

…past the suits of armour…

…and in

Chapter 11
Demnos

…the Great Hall. At the far end were two huge stone lions. In between them, just like the three gargoyles had said, was Demnos.

As we approached, the stone lions turned to flesh. Their massive teeth flashed pure white in the gloom.

Demnos peered down at us as we told
him our story. He muttered to himself
and sometimes turned and whispered to
the lions who nodded gracefully in
agreement.

When we'd
finished, he
scratched his
chin. Then his
nose. Finally
he spoke.

There is a new hospital on the east side of the city, with no gargoyle. That can be your home.

My gargoyle smiled. A lot.

Demnos wrote some strange symbols on a piece of parchment. Then he asked my gargoyle to put his footprint at the bottom.

"You must be there exactly as the sun goes down tonight or the spell will not work," he said.

Outside, we grinned like idiots. We had an hour to get across town. We could do it easily.

Then, suddenly, there was a noise. The ground moved under us…

Urrrrrk!

…and it all went horribly wrong.

Smugg held up the tracking device he'd used to follow us and smiled. I felt like a real idiot. It had been stuck in my rucksack all this time.

I tried to wriggle free, but I couldn't. The gargoyle tried to bite through the net, but it was made of hard steel.

I had to think fast. It's no use arguing with people like Rupert. You have to be cleverer than that. You need an angle.

Then I noticed the way he was looking at the gargoyle - kind of in awe.

Looks like you've really outsmarted us. You must have caught lots of strange creatures in your time.

"This is the first time I've captured anything. All I've ever wanted to do is to see a monster. A real monster," he said with a rueful smile.

I smiled too. I had seen my angle.

Chapter 13
Persuasion

"Do you realise, you and I are the only people ever to see a live gargoyle?" I said. "That's very special."

Rupert glowed with pride. You could have made toast on his cheeks.

It's a shame that won't mean anything soon.

What do you mean?

I told him that if he kept the gargoyle captive, everyone would see. Everyone would know. It would just be normal to see a gargoyle, not strange or special.

His face fell.

On the other hand, it could be our secret. We could be the only two people in the world who really know the truth.

Ten minutes later and he was practically begging to help me. There wasn't much time left. We had to get to the gargoyle's new home before sunset or we'd lose our chance. Forever.

The gargoyle was too tired to fly any more. Rupert would have to drive us.

We climbed into the back of the truck and screeched off into the dusk.

Chapter 14
Race!

We hurtled along the road, overtaking cars. In the west, the sun got lower in the sky.

Rupert's truck skidded round a corner and raced down the open road.

At first we made good speed, but then there were more and more cars. It was rush hour! There was a huge jam ahead!

EEEEEEK!

There was no turning back. It was
bumper to bumper traffic.

We'll never
make it in time!

Smugg braked hard.
I closed my eyes and felt a
claw dig into the back of my coat.

As the truck skidded to a halt we shot forward. I heard a pair of razor-sharp wings open in the twilight.

Taking off from the moving truck was like having a rocket booster.

We shot up into the air, faster than ever before.

One by one, the city
lights were coming
to life below us.

59

The hospital building was dead ahead, but we were going too fast!

The gargoyle threw his wings wide open and strained against the wind. I held on for dear life.

There it is!

We spiralled gently down to earth just as the sun was about to set.

I thought we'd done the hardest bit,
but we hadn't.

We had to say goodbye.

My gargoyle leapt up to the top of the
doorway as the last rays of the dying
sun sank below the horizon.

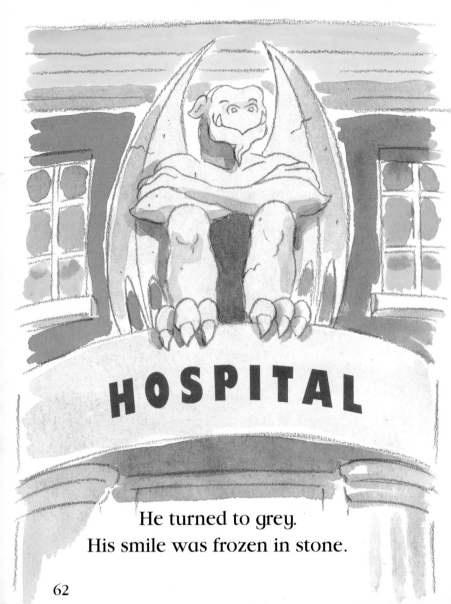

He turned to grey.
His smile was frozen in stone.

Epilogue

I go and see my gargoyle whenever I want. He looks happy in his new home and there's even a ledge to keep the rain off.

Sometimes I let Rupert Smugg come with me.

When you meet someone smarter and more skilful than you, you want to learn all you can from them.

At least, Rupert does.